Here we are again at
number 3 Tree Street.
It can't be?
Yes, it is. It's snow in the jungle.

1

What fun it will be for Bangers and Mash!
Here they come swinging down the rope.

2

They can throw snowballs.
Oh dear, Gran has just put her head
out of the window.

No, Mum, I shouldn't take the milk in
just yet. Oh dear!

4

Petal can help them make a big snowchimp.
She puts in two pieces of coal for the eyes.

5

I don't think Dad will miss his cap and pipe.
I don't think Gran will miss her scarf.

I say, Petal has found footprints.
Big footprints in the snow!

7

Could it be a lion?
Could it be Chumbo, the elephant?
Or could it be the abominable snowchimp?

8

They are digging a pit to catch
the abominable snowchimp.
We'll look round for him
while they are doing it.

There's the pond.
There's ice on it.
The duck's not very good at skating, is it?

There's Mrs Snitchnose.
She's hopping round the pond.
Her broomstick has broken down
in the cold and won't take off.

She's making big footprints. So it's her!
It's not the abominable snowchimp after all.

What a super pit!
It's all covered with branches.
But, oh, they have dug it on the garden path.

13

Now the sun's coming out.
And here comes Mum with the washing.

14

Look out, Mum!
Too late!

Where are Bangers and Mash?
Ah, there they are peeping from
behind that bush to see the
abominable snowchimp.

A good job Dad is around to help Mum out.
Those chimps have done it again.

And they are having to do the washing
again as well.
That will keep them out of mischief
for a while.

Here comes Mrs Snitchnose.
She still can't take off.

She's knocking down the chimps'
snowchimp.
What a mean trick!

20

Oh dear, she's laughing so much she's
not looking where she's going.
Shall we warn her?

She's hopping into the pit.
Oh, I bet she's hopping mad about that.
That should cool her down for a bit.

22

The chimps are busy doing the washing.
They can't help her out.
And she hasn't got her book of spells.

The sun's gone in and it's snowing again.
I think she'll make a very good snow witch,
don't you?

24